A Grain of Rice

A Grain
of Rice

Written and Illustrated by
HELENA CLARE PITTMAN

A YEARLING BOOK

Published by
Bantam Doubleday Dell Books for Young Readers
a division of
Bantam Doubleday Dell Publishing Group, Inc.
1540 Broadway
New York, New York 10036

ISBN: 0-440-41301-X

Reprinted by arrangement with Hastings House

Printed in the United States of America

April 1996

10 9 8 7 6 5 4 3

CWO

To my parents,
Florence and Jack Steinberg,
my sister, Jolene, and
my children, Theo and Galen

Once a year the Emperor of China opened his court so that even the humblest of his people could come before him. It was on one such day that Pong Lo, the son of a farmer, knelt at the Emperor's feet.

"Imperial Majesty," said Pong Lo. "I have come to ask for your daughter's hand in marriage."

The Emperor's lords were shocked.

The Princess Chang Wu, who stood near her father's throne, lowered her eyes and blushed.

"How dare you make such a request?" demanded the Emperor. His eyes were fierce and his long moustache twitched. The peasant pressed his forehead to the silken carpet.

"Forgive me, Your Majesty . . . ," he mumbled.

"Speak up!" commanded the Emperor.

Pong Lo lifted his head. ". . . but I am more than qualified to be her husband!" he declared.

The lords giggled.

2

"Qualified!" cried the outraged Emperor gripping his sword. "Such boldness qualifies you to lose your head!"

"But it is my head which qualifies me!" replied Pong Lo. "It is wise and quick and more than a little clever, and would make me as fine a prince as China has ever seen."

"Prince!" shrieked the Emperor. "A peasant cannot be a prince! A prince must come from noble blood!" His moustache twitched madly.

"My blood may not be noble, Your Majesty," returned Pong Lo. "But it, too, is clever."

"What do you mean?" the Emperor demanded.

"Though it has to find its way through 70,000 miles of veins," answered the peasant quietly, "it never fails to reach my heart."

Now the lords smiled behind their fans at Pong Lo's skillful answer. Princess Chang Wu's black eyes sparkled.

"Enough of this!" growled the Emperor, raising his sword.

"Father, wait!" The scent of lotus blossoms filled the air as the Princess rushed to the Emperor's side. "Don't be hasty, Father," she begged. "The young man is clever. He could be useful!"

"He will be useful when his clever tongue is no longer flapping in his head!" the Emperor snapped.

"Father," the Princess coaxed, "since he is so good with numbers perhaps he can work in the storeroom."

The Emperor eyed the peasant shrewdly. Pong Lo's head was once again pressed to the floor. He looked so humble.

The Princess smiled hopefully at her father and placed her hand gently upon his. Her touch was like the brush of silk stirring in a summer breeze. Suddenly the Emperor's cares felt lighter.

Sighing, the Emperor sat down again. "My gentle daughter," he said, looking fondly at Chang Wu, "for your sake I will spare him. But he will have to prove his worth. He can scrub the storeroom. If he works hard he can stay."

So Pong Lo was given a place to sleep in the farthest corner of the palace, and he was put to work. He cleaned the deep, wooden storeroom shelves. He washed the grain bins and scrubbed the stone floor, and polished it carefully with a wax he made himself. It gleamed as it never had before.

"How do you do that?" asked the Imperial Storeroom Keeper.

"Just an old family recipe," Pong Lo answered cheerfully. And when he had finished that, instead of going off to drink tea or sit under a tree, he helped the other storeroom servants, sorting the grains that came from the Emperor's fields. The expression on his face was always pleasant and his step was light. As he worked he often hummed a merry tune which was so delightful that the other servants couldn't help but sing with him.

Pong Lo did everything so well that the Imperial Storeroom Keeper put him in

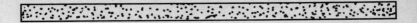

charge of the shelves. He stored the beans and dried fruits. He shelled the nuts and stacked the pickled eggs and vegetables. He laid the teas and spices carefully in their boxes, and kept count of everything. When something was in short supply he always noticed. He knew where to get even the strangest ingredients and at the best price. He knew so much about rare herbs and spices that before long the Emperor's cooks were seeking his advice.

The Imperial Storeroom Keeper told the Steward. The Steward told the Minister of Palace Affairs. The Minister told the Chamberlain. The Chamberlain told the Prime Minister and the Prime Minister told the Emperor.

12

"Hmmm," said the Emperor, stroking his moustache. "Clever indeed! Make him Imperial Assistant to the Imperial Storeroom Keeper."

"Clever is the word!" the servants whispered.

But as if that weren't enough, when his long day in the storeroom ended, Pong Lo asked to help in the kitchen.

At first he sliced and diced and chopped, whistling as he worked. He stirred and sampled, and offered a pleasant suggestion or two. Soon he was salting and seasoning until the fragrance of his sauces steamed through the palace. The Imperial Cooks whistled along with Pong Lo's lively tunes. The Imperial Kitchen Maid trilled a chorus. The waiters stepped jauntily as they carried their trays from the kitchen to the Emperor's table, and everyone from lords to servants looked forward as never before to the next meal—even the Imperial Kitchen Cat, who purred loudly over the leftovers. Pong Lo's recipes were delicious!

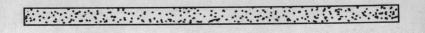

15

The Emperor, who loved to eat, was delighted. "Excellent!" he remarked to the Princess night after night over dinner. "Make him Imperial Assistant to the Imperial Cook as well!" he told the Prime Minister. Pong Lo was moved to a small room, in keeping with his new position.

Princess Chang Wu listened carefully for any word of Pong Lo. She couldn't forget his handsome face, his cleverness, and his bravery before her father. At every excuse she passed the kitchen or the storeroom to catch a glimpse of him. The smell of the lotus blossoms she wore in her hair followed her, and told Pong Lo that she was near. Then his heartbeat quickened and his song sounded sweeter. Sometimes their eyes met and they shared a smile.

"You have grown so lovely, my dear," said the Emperor to the Princess one day. "The time is coming to find a husband for you. In the summer I shall invite all the young nobles of China to the palace and I will choose from among them."

The Princess looked sad and hurried away.

As the days passed and summer came, the palace bustled with activity in preparation for the arrival of China's most excellent young noblemen. But Chang Wu seemed not to care. With no hope of marrying Pong Lo she grew sadder and sadder until at last she only stayed in bed. Her black eyes lost their sparkle and her cheeks became pale.

21

The Emperor's physicians shook their heads. Their potions were useless. Day after day the Princess lay with her face to the window. She wouldn't speak or eat. When the Emperor came to sit near her bed, she only wept. Heartsick, the Emperor issued a proclamation: Anyone in China who could cure the Princess would be handsomely rewarded.

Peasants and nobles alike made their way to the royal city. They tried berries and ointments. They tried chants and spells. Nothing worked. The Princess grew steadily worse.

But late into the night, a light burned in Pong Lo's room. The fragrance of herbs drifted into the corridor as he crushed and pounded and brewed the leaves and roots he knew so well. One morning, as the Princess lay dying, he appeared before the

Emperor. His face was strained from care and lack of sleep but his gaze was steady.

"Your Majesty," he said. "Here is the potion that will cure the Princess Chang Wu." He held out a tiny bottle filled with green liquid.

"How can you be sure?" asked the despairing Emperor.

"The recipe has been in my family for hundreds of years," said Pong Lo. "It will cure the disease if the heart is willing. But you must tell the Princess that it comes from me."

"If she lives you shall have anything you want!" cried the Emperor, and clutching the bottle, he hurried to the Princess' bed.

Chang Wu opened her eyes and looked at her father with a sad smile. A tear fell to her pillow like a petal from a fading blossom. The Emperor thought his heart would break.

"Take this, my child," he said. "It comes from Pong Lo."

"Pong Lo!" exclaimed the Princess with a weak cry. A flush came over her pale face.

"My precious one," said the Emperor sadly. "If it makes you well I will grant him anything he asks."

"Will you father?" cried the Princess. "Will you really?" And without another word she drank down Pong Lo's potion.

The next morning the palace was alive with the news: The Princess had eaten breakfast! By the following afternoon she was sitting in a chair by the window. Overcome with joy and relief the Emperor called his lords together to celebrate with him in his court, and he summoned Pong Lo.

"Honorable Pong Lo," he said. "I owe my happiness to you. Name the reward and it shall be yours."

"There is only one thing I have ever desired, Your Majesty," said Pong Lo, "And that is the hand of the Princess Chang Wu."

The Emperor's smile vanished and he tooked troubled. "Good Pong Lo," he said. "I am saddened by your request, for you have more than proven your worth. But still I cannot grant the Princess' hand to a humble peasant. There must be something else that will satisfy you."

Pong Lo lowered his eyes sadly. "That is not possible, Your Majesty," he said quietly, and for a long moment he seemed to be thinking. "But perhaps there *is* something else," he said at last.

"Anything!" cried the Emperor.

"A grain of rice," said the peasant.

"A grain of rice?" repeated the Emperor. He glanced at his lords, but they had long since stopped laughing at Pong Lo. The Emperor lowered his voice and leaned forward. "Surely there must be something more?"

"No, Your Majesty," said Pong Lo.

"That's nonsense!" exclaimed the Emperor. "Ask me for fine silks, the grandest room in the palace, a stable full of stallions—they shall be yours!"

"If I cannot marry the Princess then one grain of rice is all I desire."

"That is preposterous," said the Emperor. "Take a chest of gold. A herd of oxen!"

"A grain of rice," said Pong Lo.

"A servant of your own!" cried the Emperor.

"A grain of rice will do," said Pong Lo. "But if His Majesty insists, he may double the amount every day for a hundred days."

"It is ridiculous!" scoffed the Emperor, twisting his moustache between his fingers and eying Pong Lo. "But it is granted."

That very afternoon a grain of rice was delivered to Pong Lo's room. It rested on a tiny cushion, in the center of a silver bird's nest. If the peasant insisted on being humble, the Emperor could at least be generous.

34

With Princess Chang Wu's health improving every day, life in the palace returned to normal. Pong Lo went back to his work in the kitchen.

On the second day a fine china cup, painted with delicate pink flowers, was left at Pong Lo's door. Two grains of rice had been placed inside.

On the third day, four grains were left, resting neatly on the back of an alabaster swan. Pong Lo picked it up on his way back from the kitchen and put it in the corner of his room—next to the silver bird's nest and the fine china cup.

On the fourth day, eight grains of rice were left in an enameled bowl. Pong Lo admired its simple beauty.

On the fifth day, sixteen grains arrived on a golden plate.

Thirty-two grains of rice were brought on the sixth day, nestled delicately in the mouth of a carved dragonfish. The corner of Pong Lo's room was getting cluttered.

Sixty-four grains, resting in a small boat made of precious stones, appeared on the seventh day.

On the eighth, a jade box arrived. It held one hundred and twenty-eight grains of rice.

Two hundred and fifty-six grains of rice were delivered on the ninth day. They lay on an ivory tray.

"Hmmm," remarked the Emperor on the tenth day. "Five hundred and twelve grains of rice! It will be more than a thousand tomorrow!"

By the twelfth day the grains of rice numbered two thousand and forty eight. They were sent to Pong Lo in a box covered with embroidered silk. Pong Lo's room was crowded with gold and jewels and ivory and alabaster, and littered with grains of rice. There was hardly room left for Pong Lo. The Emperor had him moved to a small house on the palace grounds.

On the eighteenth day two oxen arrived at the new house. Each carried two ebony chests. One-hundred-thirty-one-thousand-and-seventy-two grains of rice were in the chests.

"Five-hundred-twenty-four-thousand-two-hundred-and-eighty-eight grains of rice!" exclaimed the Emperor on the twentieth day. "Tomorrow it will be more than a million!" His anxious fingers pulled at his moustache and he summoned the Imperial Mathematician.

The mathematician pushed and pulled at the ebony beads of his abacus and he scribbled with his brush on a paper scroll. "Imperial Majesty, at this rate, in ten days there will be no rice left in the palace!"

The emperor paced and thought. "Then we shall have to get more!"

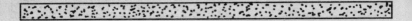

On the twenty-fifth day, sixteen-million-seven-hundred-seventy-seven-thousand-two-hundred-and-sixteen grains of rice were delivered in brocaded sacks, carried on the backs of twenty-five of the Emperor's Imperial Horses. On the twenty-sixth day the Emperor issued

a proclamation: For every bushel of rice brought to the palace he would pay one piece of gold. Rice poured in from all over China.

Pong Lo grew richer every day, the Emperor grew more anxious. How could this go on for a hundred days! Again he summoned his mathematician. The mathematician's fingers flew and the abacus beads clacked.

"Your Majesty!" he cried. "By next month that young man will own all the rice in China!"

The Emperor was beside himself. But he had given his word before his Court. "Then we shall have to get more!"

48

Five-hundred-thirty-six-million-eight-hundred-and-seventy-thousand-nine-hundred-and-twelve grains of rice were delivered to Pong Lo on the thirtieth day. It took forty servants to carry them in huge brass urns.

By the thirty-fifth day it was clear that Pong Lo would have to move again. The Emperor gave him his summer palace.

Ships were sent across the ocean to buy more rice. Every day new servants had to be found. From morning until night they counted out grains of rice. The matter of Princess Chang Wu's marriage was postponed indefinitely.

On the fortieth day, a caravan of one hundred elephants was sent to the summer palace. On their backs were loaded great trunks carved of rosewood and

inlaid with mother of pearl. Altogether they held five-hundred-forty-nine-billion-seven-hundred-fifty-five-million-eight-hundred-and-thirteen-thousand-eight-hundred-and-eighty-eight grains of rice!

The Emperor watched the procession gloomily from his balcony. The mathematician worked his abacus, sitting in a tangle of scrolls at the Emperor's feet. He scribbled and muttered while the beads of the abacus clicked and clacked.

"My figures must be wrong!" he shouted at last. "There couldn't be that much rice in the world!" So he started his calculations again. He stammered and swore and spluttered and broke his brushes and tore up paper and grew more and more frustrated until finally the Emperor had to send him away.

Alone in his private chamber the Emperor sat with his head in his hands. Soon his treasury would be empty.

He called his lords to his Court. And he summoned Pong Lo.

The young man arrived at the palace dressed richly in the clothes he had bought with his rice. Twenty servants of his own attended him. His step was light and the expression on his face was as good-natured as ever. He bowed to the

Emperor and smiled at the Princess, who stood in her place at the Emperor's side. Chang Wu's eyes sparkled as she returned Pong Lo's smile.

"Greetings, most honorable Pong Lo," The Emperor began. "You are looking well. It has been some time since we have met."

"Thank you, Your Majesty," said Pong Lo. "To be precise, it has been forty days."

"Only forty days," lamented the Emperor. "Life at the summer palace is pleasant, I hope?"

"The view is wonderful," returned Pong Lo. "And my days are filled with activity. Counting, storing, selling rice…"

"Yes!" the Emperor interrupted. "They must be. I imagine you are growing tired of rice?" he asked hopefully.

"Oh no, Your Majesty," said Pong Lo. "It will make a fine barrier against the winter wind. And there are so many things to be made with it. Rice paper, rice wine, rice cakes, rice noodles, rice syrup — I could go on and on."

The Emperor looked gloomy. "I do not doubt it," he said. "Things have not gone as well for me however. I have been having a problem with my daughter Chang Wu. The mere mention of marriage sends her into a fit of melancholy."

The Princess blushed.

The Emperor shifted uncomfortably on his throne. "Honorable Pong Lo," he began again. "You have become a rich man."

Pong Lo smiled modestly.

"Richer than any nobleman in China," said the Emperor. "At last you can care for my daughter as a Princess should be cared for. I have therefore decided to make you a Prince and grant you her hand in marriage." Here the Emperor leaned forward and lowered his voice. "But no more rice!" he said.

The clever Pong Lo bowed again. "I humbly accept your offer, Father," he said.

A sigh went through the Court. "When is dinner?" someone whispered.

61

Pong Lo and Chang Wu were married. The wedding feast was wonderful, its preparation supervised by the new Prince

himself. There was bean soup, and bean
curd. Bean paste and sprouted beans.
There were barley cakes and barley

candies. Pressed duck and steamed dumplings. Fish with millet and pheasant with millet. There were wheat noodles, potato noodles, corn noodles, fried noodles. But—out of respect for the Emperor's feelings—not a single grain of rice.

The Emperor lived to be an old man. At his death, Prince Pong Lo and Princess Chang Wu inherited his kingdom. They lived happily, and ruled wisely, all their days.

65

ABOUT THE AUTHOR/ILLUSTRATOR

HELENA CLARE PITTMAN is the author of *Once When I Was Scared* and the author-illustrator of *Gift of the Willows, Miss Hindy's Cats, Where Will You Swim Tonight,* and the Gerald books. She lives on Long Island, New York with her two children and three cats.